SINGING BOWLS

Other books by Binkey Kok Publications bv

Dirk Schellberg
Didgeridoo
Ritual Origins and Playing Techniques
ISBN 90-74597-13-0

Eva Rudy Jansen
The Book of Buddhas
Ritual Symbolism Used
on Buddhist Statuary and Ritual Objects
ISBN 90-74597-02-5

Eva Rudy Jansen
The Book of Hindu Imagery
The Gods and their Symbols
ISBN 90-74597-07-6 PBK
ISBN 90-74597-10-6 CLOTH

Ab Williams
The Complete Book of Chinese Health Balls
Background and Use of the Health Balls
ISBN 90-74597-28-9

George Hulskramer
The Life of Buddha
Prince Siddharta to Buddha
ISBN 90-74597-17-3

Töm Klöwer
The Joy of Drumming
Drums and Percussion Instruments from around the World
ISBN 90-74597-13-9

Anneke Huyser
Singing Bowl
Exercises for Personal Harmony
ISBN 90-74597-39-4

SINGING BOWLS

A PRACTICAL HANDBOOK
OF INSTRUCTION AND USE

by

Eva Rudy Jansen

Binkey Kok Publications bv, Havelte, Holland

CIP-DATA KONINKLIJKE BIBLIOTHEEK, DEN HAAG

Jansen, Eva Rudy

Singing Bowls: a practical handbook of instruction and use / Eva Rudy Jansen; [ill. Bert Wieringa ... et al.; transl. from the Dutch by Tony Langam ... et al.]. Diever: Binkey Kok. – Ill.
Transl. of Klankschalen: werking en gebruik. – Diever; Binkey Kok, 1990. – With index.
ISBN 90-74597-01-7
Subject headings: singing bowls / spirituality / music therapy.

Published and © by Binkey Kok Publications bv
Havelte, Holland, Fax 31 521-591925
www.binkeykok.com
E-mail: info@binkeykok.com

Printed and bound in the Netherlands.
Artwork and lay-out: Eva Rudy Jansen
Cover design: Jaap Koning.

Distributed in the U.S.A. by Red Wheel/Weiser
Orderphone: 1-800-423-7087

© 1992 by Binkey Kok.
© Thirteenth printing 2004 by Binkey Kok Publications bv

To
Amitabha
the Lord of Meditation and Intuition

Contents

Introduction IX

Part 1 **Getting Acquainted** 1
The meeting of East and West 3
Masters of sound 6
Notes 12

Part 2 **History** 15
The origin of things 17
Ringing stones and fountain bowls 20
Singing bowls, chalices and food dishes... 22

Part 3 **How Singing Bowls Work** 29
External characteristics 31
Sound is shape 34
Natural harmonies 36
Synchronization and inner massage 38
Shamanism and brainwaves 40

Part 4 **Practice** 43
The individual sound is always unique 45
A way to choose 47
Tools 51
Signposts in a magic land 55
An open heart and an open mind 61
Therapeutic use 62

Part 5   **Tingshaws, Bell and Dorje** 65
Tingshaws 67
Bell and dorje 73

Conclusion 87

Sources and Bibliography 91

Introduction

A journey of a thousand miles begins
with a single step

Lao Tse
(Tao Te Ching)

The large metal bowl sits heavily in my hand. I strike the rim gently with a felt-tipped beater. A humming, singing sound envelops me. The deep, throbbing undertones gradually change into undulating overtones. I strike the bowl again, and then again and again. The more I strike, the more the room in which I am sitting is filled with sound. The sound calms me. I gradually lose an awareness of time and place. I am living in the sound and the sound is living in me.

The singing bowl sound is affecting more and more people in the same way. The phenomenon of the 'singing bowl' (or 'Tibetan bells', as they are also sometimes called) is becoming increasingly well known. The wonderful singing sounds of these bowls are being discovered by more and more people through concerts and through the tapes and records which have been produced, and many people would like to develop their interest by acquiring one of these bowls themselves.

With an increasing awareness of the sound of the singing bowl comes the mystery of where the sound originates and what is its true purpose. The few people who really know something about Tibetan singing bowls all have different views. Some have worked with the bowls for many years, some have travelled the border states of the Himalayas, while others have made detailed studies of the origin of these unique sounds. On some points there is agreement; on others, opinions differ totally. What is an unsuspecting amateur of the singing bowl, fascinated by the sound and curious about its origin and use, to make of this?

After months of study, investigation and discussion with the few experts that I could find in the Netherlands, I have come to one definite conclusion: everyone should make up his own mind. The experience of the sound itself is and will always be the most important factor. In this book I will try to bring together the different views on singing bowls. However, there are bound to be some loose ends. In addition, I will try to explain the phenomenon of sound in greater depth – both its effect in general, and the effect of the sounds of singing bowls in particular. People often think that the physical and spiritual effect of singing bowls is a matter of suggestion, or that you must in some way 'believe' in them in order to experience their influences, yet no one would suggest that you have to believe in music in order to hear it. Sound is a physical phenomenon, and the perception of sound takes place in accordance with principles that can be explained in physical and biological terms. That means it is possible to describe exactly how sound works, why it is the way it is, and how it produces its particular effects. These natural laws are, in fact, the secret which lies behind everything and which every religion tries to explain. It is striking that the various explanations often use similar fundamental principles, sometimes corroborated by recent scientific discoveries. Nevertheless, even the laws of nature have a secret core. Secrets guard themselves well and eventually only reveal themselves to people who are prepared to find their own way through the labyrinth of phenomena and explanations. The path they follow will only lead to an understanding of the mystery through their own experience and intuition.

I do not claim that this book gives a complete picture or, that it is in some way 'the truth'. At best, it is a summary of opinions, ideas and phenomena. However, I do hope that it will serve as a guide to the reader – especially the part of the book which deals with the practical aspects of finding a singing bowl for yourself and getting to know it better.

The information on the use of sound in meditation, healing and prayer, is completed by the addition of a chapter about character and purpose of tingshaws, Tibetan bells and dorje.

The particular sources of the ideas, statements and information given in this book are not always acknowledged within the text. This is not done out of a lack of respect, but simply so that the text can be read easily without too many distracting details. A complete summary of the written and verbal sources used is given at the end of the book. However, I would like to acknowledge and thank those who have been the most important sources. In their own way, they have all been my teachers, not only for this book but also on the path of my life. They are:

Joska Soos, a Hungarian shaman, who lives in Antwerp, and introduced me to the singing bowls ten years ago. Since then, he has continued to teach me. He has taught me about shamanism and the shamanistic use of sound and singing bowls. He is the only person I know who was actually told some of the secrets of the singing bowls by Tibetan monks at least untill after the first publication of this book. Then I met with mr. Phuntsog Wangyal of the Tibet Foundation in London, who confirmed everything I had learned so far about the use of the bowls in ritual meditation and prayer.

I first met **Dries Langeveld**, chief editor of the magazine BRES, when I began to write this book. He proved to be an exceptional teacher in this field. He has made his extensive knowledge of the origins, background and use of singing bowl available to me, and has shared his own ideas on the singing bowls and taught me some special applications and ways of using them.

Hans de Back is a soundtherapist and friend and colleague in sound and story-telling. He passed on his knowledge and experience of singing bowls and tingshaws to me.

Danny Becher and Lisa Borstlap set up the Institute of Sound and Form together and did many years of research into the connection between the two. They allowed me to make use of their wide knowledge of the therapeutic uses of singing bowls and the wonderful world of vibrations.

Erik Bruijn, a writer, traveller in Tibet, and expert on Buddhism, enthusiastically allowed me to use a passage from his book 'Tantra, Yoga and Meditation'.

The publishing company, **Sirius and Siderius**, generously gave me permission to use the wonderful story about 'The Master in Sound' told by the explorer Alexandra David-Neel in her book 'Tibet, Land of Bandits, Priests and Demons'.

Margot Kool and Koosje van der Kolk, of the Tibetan-Buddhistic Study- and Meditationcentre Maytreya Institute (Gelugpa tradition) shared important knowledge about function and use of the Tibetan bell with me.

Lama Gawang of the Tibetan-Buddhistic Centre Karma Deleg Chöhpel Ling (Kagyu tradition) took me beyond knowledge and showed me the true meaning of the Lamaïstic use of bell and dorje: tab-sherab.

Finally, **Binkey Kok**, a lover of singing bowls, who also imports them from Tibet, fired me with his enthusiasm and gave me the opportunity to experiment in his storehouse so that I could find out and experience for myself everything that I had learned about from others.

All my teachers agreed on this particular point: you can always talk about sound but in the end it is one's own personal experience of sound that is the real way in – first to the sound itself and from there, into the inner being. Where, in the heart of the labyrinth, there are many, many worlds to be found and you can recognize them all if you learn to differentiate between the different sounds of a singing bowl – if you listen closely!

Part 1
Getting Acquainted

There is nothing in the world that does not
speak to us. Everything and everybody
reveals their own nature, character, and
secrets continuously. The more we open up
our inner senses, the more we can
understand the voice of everything.

Hazrat Inayat Khan
(Music and Mysticism)

The Meeting of East and West

Before the beginning of this century, travel abroad was the privilege of merchants, soldiers, missionaries, anthropologists and the rich in search of adventure, in roughly that order. They would return home with reports that were coloured by their own view of the world. Thus, for many years, people who lived in foreign lands were usually described as 'barbarians, savages, heathens' and their views on life, their philosophies and religions were often labelled as 'superstitious', 'idolatrous' and sometimes even 'childish'. However, there were some travellers who learned to respect the beliefs of the cultures they visited. Some travellers, such as the Frenchwoman Alexandra David-Neel, who became a Buddhist, even adopted such beliefs as the guiding principles of their own lives. However, people like this were the exception rather than the rule.

In the 1960s a fundamental change took place. A new youth culture spread from California throughout the western world in the form of the hippy movement, advocating flower power, spiritual growth, peace on earth and a new way for people to live together. With characters such as the Beatles leading the way, people began to turn their attention to the East and even travelled there. They went East not with a bag full of money and looking for material wealth, but hitch-hiking, and in search of new spiritual values.

East and West came together in the ashrams of India and the mountains of Nepal. This time, the Eastern people were the teachers and the Westerners were the humble, curious students. They realized they had not only found new ways of thinking and new spiritual paths, but had also stumbled upon an unknown world of sound. It is possible that the significance and application of sound, which were still common in the East, were once known about in the West, but they were either completely destroyed at the time of the Druids in Europe, or the Indians in the Americas, or, in modern times, have been overshadowed by the inflexible rules of rational thinking. One of the 'sound phenomena' that the 'spiritual tourists' discovered south of the Himalayas, and which later gradually appeared in Europe and the United States, was the singing bowl. These were round metal bowls of various sizes, some polished, some matt, a golden or occasionally almost black colour. They always produce a wonderful singing sound when they are tapped, struck or rubbed. Many people would experience this sound in the same way that Binkey Kok describes.

'I have travelled to the Far East regularly for the past 20 years. About ten or twelve years ago I saw a bronze bowl that was being sold by a Tibetan from whom I occasionally bought jewellery. I asked him what it was. He said it was a 'singing bowl', and that was the first time I had ever heard of such a thing. He tapped the bowl with his fingernail and I heard a familiar and at the same time, quite unfamiliar sound. I was hooked. I wanted a bowl like this. The Tibetan was not prepared to sell his bowl, but a day or two later he had another bowl for me. He refused to tell me where it came from. As soon as you start to make enquiries, you are told that the bowls are just dishes for eating or household articles.'

The fact that it was a Tibetan who sold the bowl could just be chance. I have never heard of anyone else who has either heard or bought a singing bowl in Tibet. That does not mean that they do not exist in Tibet. The Tibetan merchant who sold the bowl could just as well be a sign that singing bowls do also actually come from Tibet. If this is the case, they would have appeared in the West as a result of the Chinese invasion of Tibet in 1951. Initially, the Chinese left the lamas and their monasteries more or less alone. But then they systematically began to destroy the monasteries and thousands of Tibetan monks died, while most of the survivors fled the country. It is said that more than 90% of the Tibetan monasteries and temples were razed to the ground.

The monks obviously could not carry much with them when they fled from the Chinese and later, in dire poverty, they were forced to sell some of the possessions which they had managed to take out of

Tibet. In this way the religious artifacts of the lamas appeared on the market stalls of Nepal and Northern India. It is possible that the bowls which are now known in the West as singing bowls were amongst these belongings. The question as to whether or not these bowls were originally singing bowls will be discussed later in this book. Joska Soos's experience seems to prove that they are, in fact, the originals. In the early 1980s he went to a lama monastery in England for an extended retreat. The lamas he met listened to him, studied his horoscope and advised him that he should become involved with sound if he wished to accelerate his spiritual development.

'They took me to a small room and there were the bowls. I listened to them. Afterwards they presented me with some bowls. I did not have to go on a retreat. I merely had to intensify my path, immersing myself in the sounds. I did this very attentively, without forcing myself. Slowly it came to me, the whole universe opened up. Amongst the lamas themselves, these bowls are only used in secret rituals by those who are acknowledged masters in sound. They have learned to sing the ritual songs and play the ritual instruments correctly. They use the singing bowls in secret and only for themselves, not in public, and not even for other monks. It is strictly forbidden to talk about the rituals or the singing bowls themselves. This is because a knowledge of sound carries with it great power. It allows one to travel without moving. It is possible to come into contact with planets and their spirits, with the subterranean kingdom of Aggartha and with Shamballah, the earthly centre of the Immortals. If you ask a lama with a singing bowl in his hands, whether it is true that they are used for psychic, psychological and physical purposes, he will smile and reply: 'Perhaps'.'

Masters of sound

Secrets keep themselves. If Joska Soos's experience is not an isolated one, if there are 'masters of sound' working with singing bowls behind closed doors in other Tibetan monasteries, they have certainly kept their secret well – at least as regards the singing bowls. With regard to the 'mastery of sound' there are testimonies from other witnesses. For example, in his book, 'Tantra, Yoga and Meditation, the Tibetan way to Enlightenment', Erik Bruijn describes the symbolic composition of the Tibetan temple orchestra in the following way.

'(...) The sounds produced by the musical instruments form the counterpart to the inner sounds that can be observed in the body in a state of total stillness. If one shuts out the sounds from the outside world, one can hear the murmur ofthe circulation of the blood, and after while, also the rhythm of one's own heartbeat. Because they are able to direct their concentration inwards for a long time, experienced monks and yogis are able to clearly detect the most subtle vibrations generated by organic processes in their own bodies. The characteristics of the sounds they hear are described with great accuracy in Tibetan aesthetics on music. These texts describe singing, beating, thumping, clashing, tinkling, complaining and blaring sounds. The musical sounds that serve as the counterpart to these organic sounds are produced by the instruments which constitute the temple orchestra. The 'rustling' is represented by the sound of the conch, the 'beating' is produced by hand drums, the 'thumping' by the big drums, the 'clanging' by cymbals, the 'tinkling' by bells and the 'groaning' by the sound of the shawms.'

In 1983, a group of Dutch artists and musicians co-operated together on a project in which body sounds, such as the heartbeat and the circulation of the blood, were amplified and reproduced as a theatrical piece. This was presented as 'an audible journey through the body'. Erik, who attended this performance, noted how accurately the Tibetan monks reproduced the body's sounds. He comments: 'What I heard was precisely the sound of the Tibetan temple orchestra.'

Alexandra David-Neel describes another wonderful experience with sound in her book 'Tibet, Bandits, Priests and Demons'. When she entered the temple in the Bön monastery of Tesmon, the service that was being conducted was rudely interrupted. While a lama was busy with a *kyilkhor*, a magic diagram, and sacred cakes, called *tormas*, one of her bearers entered the temple, clearly indicating that he was not very impressed by the sacred rituals. He was ordered away by the monks. Objecting and cursing violently he insulted the lamas by shouting out that the tormas were only made of momo dough (bread dough).

'(...) Then, as the man came forward, the *bonpo* (1) grasped a *chang*, (2) which was standing next to him, and swung it around. Strange, savage sounds filled the room with a tidal wave of vibrations that pierced my ears. The disrespectful peasant screamed and staggered back with his arms held up as though he was warding off something threatening.

'Get out', the lama repeated again.

The other bearers grabbed their friend and rushed out of the temple, greatly disturbed.

Bong! Bong! continued the drum. The accompanying *bonpo* returned unperturbed, sat in front of the *kyilkhor*, and continued the muffled singing and chanting.

What had happened? I hadn't noticed anything, except for that extraordinary sound. I went outside and asked my bearers. The troublemaker who had disturbed the sacred ritual had lost his bravado.

'It was a snake. I tell you', he said, nodding to the others who sat around him. 'A snake of fire came out of the *chang*.'

'What? Did you really see a snake of fire?' I asked. Is that why you recoiled?'

'Didn't you see it?' they replied. 'It came out of the *chang* when the lama beat upon it.'

'You must have dreamt it,' I said. 'I didn't see anything.' 'We didn't see the snake, but we did see flashes of light shoot out of the *chang*,' the other bearers interjected.

In fact, they had all been witnesses to a miracle. Only I, an unworthy foreigner, had been blind. (...)'

The writer decided to apologize to the lama, and he accepted her apology amicably.

'(...) The obligations of politeness had been fulfilled. The *bonpo* remained silent. I had to leave but I was still intrigued by the bizarre sound I had heard and the extraordinary vision the villagers had seen. Inadvertently, I looked at the *chang* that had been the start of this whole phantamasgoria. The lama read my thoughts easily. 'Would you like to hear the sound again?' he asked, with a rather mocking smile.

'Yes, Kouchog, I would very much like to, if you have no objections. The instrument has a quite remarkable sound. Would you mind letting me hear it again?'

'You can play it yourself,' he replied, and handed me the *chang*. 'I haven't had any practice,' I told him.

Certainly, the sound I produced sounded nothing like the sound I had heard. 'I do not have your skill, Kouchog,' I said to the lama as I gave the instrument back to him. 'No snakes of fire came out of your *chang*.'

The *bonpo* looked at me questioningly. Was he pretending not to understand or did he actually not understand?

'Yes,' I continued, 'the rude man who shouted at you claims that he saw a snake of fire coming out of the *chang* that was trying to swoop down on him. The others with him saw either flashes of light or sparks.'

'That is the power of the *zoung* (3) that I cast,' declared the lama emphatically. Speaking more softly he said: 'The sound creates shapes and beings.. the sound inspires them.'

I think he was quoting from a text. I remarked that the people from India, the *tchirolpa*, (4) also made such claims.

I hoped that by saying this, I would encourage him to explain his point of view and to speak about the religious path that he followed, and I went on: 'However, some people believe that the power of thought transcends that of sound.'

'There are also lamas who believe that,' answered the *bonpo*. 'Everyone has his own point of view. Ways of working differ. I am a master of sound. Through sound I can kill what lives and bring back to life what is dead...'

'*Kouchog*, these two things, life and death, do they really exist as opposites, completely different from each other?'

'Are you a *Dzotchénpa* (5)?' asked the man opposite me.

'One of my teachers was a *Dzogtchénpa*,' I replied evasively.

The *bonpo* then fell silent. I wanted to bring the conversation back to the question of life and death and to find out what his theories on the subject were, but his silence was not very encouraging. Should I interpret it as a polite way of showing me that it was time I left?

But then the lama mumbled something indistinctly, took hold of the *chang* and made it ring a few times.

It was wonderful! Instead of hearing the terrifying sound he had made earlier or the rather disharmonious sounds I had produced myself, I heard a melodious carillon of silver bells. How was that possible? Was this *bonpo* simply an artist who had withdrawn from the world, and could anyone, given enough practice, achieve such different effects on such a primitive instrument as the *chang*, or must I accept that he was a 'master of sound' as he so proudly declared? My desire to continue the conversation with the lama increased. Would I succeed in getting him to explain to me the mystery of the *chang*? (...)'

Unfortunately for Alexandra the conversation was broken off at that point, and she was only able to continue the next day when she invited the lama to have tea with her. The conversation began with polite enquiries from the lama about India.

'(...) I controlled myself and tried to satisfy his curiosity, hoping that I would have an opportunity to ask questions myself. The opportunity arose when he spoke about the *doubthobs* (6) of India.

'It isn't necessary to go to India to meet people with these powers,' I said to him.

'I believe that you yourself proved that to me yesterday evening. The Hindus also revere Tibet as a sanctuary of great and wise men, and they believe that the magicians who live in Tibet are more powerful than their own magicians.'

'That is possible,' replied the *bonpo*. 'I have never been to India. You're thinking about the *chang*, aren't you? Why do you attach such importance to something so trivial? Sound has other mysteries.

Sound is produced by all beings and all things, even those which appear to have no soul. Every being and thing has its own sound, but this sound changes depending upon on the state of the being or thing producing the sound at any particular moment. How does that work? Everything is a collection of atoms (*rdul phra*) which dance and produce sounds by their movements.

It is said that in the beginning the wind created the *gyatams* (7), the basis of our world, by a spinning movement. This movement of the wind was melodious and it was this kind of sound that combined the form and the matter of the *gyatam* (8) to form a whole. The first *gyatams* sang, and from them emerged shapes that, in turn, produced others through the power of the sound that they had made. This applies not only to the past but is still true today. Every atom ceaselessly sings its song, constantly creating coarse and fine substances. And just as there are creative sounds, there are also destructive sounds which cause matter to disintegrate. Anyone who can produce both sounds can create and destroy at will. In fact, a *doubthob* who can produce the basic destructive sound which lies at the root of all destructive sounds (9), should be able to wipe out this world and all the worlds of the gods, up to the world of the mighty 'Thirtythree' (10) of which the Buddhists speak.'

After this explanation he said goodbye, expressing the wish that the following day would be fine and that I should have a successful journey. His explanation of this rather doubtful theory was certainly interesting, but it did not, in any way, clarify what I called the 'mystery of the chang'.'

Alexandra David-Neel found these theories obscure, but the lama's story has been told in different ways all over the world, and his explanation about moving atoms creating sounds comes surprisingly close to the theories of modern atomic physics...

Notes

The italics used in Alexandra David Neel's story are just as the author used them. In the following notes I have quoted only the parts that are necessary for a proper understanding of the text.

1. A follower of the Bön religion.
2. The *chang* (written as *'gchang'*) is a musical instrument that is especially used by *bonpos*. It is roughly the same shape as a cymbal, with the edges bent inward and it has a clapper. It is played with the clapper pointing upwards like an upturned bell.
3. Written as *'gzungs'*: something that grips, holds onto. A magic formula. The Sanskrit equivalent is *dharani mantra*.
4. Written as *'phyirolpa'*: outsiders, meaning people who are not Buddhists, followers of another faith. It refers here specifically to the Brahmin Hindus.
5. Belonging to the *Dzogtchen* sect (written as *'rdzogstchen'*): 'great fulfillment'. The most recently established Tibetan sect. (...)
6. Written as *'grubthob'*: someone who possesses supernatural powers. The Tibetan equivalent of the Sanskrit *Siddha* or *Siddhi purucha*.
7. Refers to the Tibetan creation myths, in which the 'wind' (*rlung*, pronounced *'lung'*) is not the wind as we know it, but the movement of the first forms, the *gyatams* (written as *'rgya Pram'* or *'rgua gram'*). The Lamaïsts depict these *gyatams* as *dorjis* intertwined in the shape of the cross, whilst the *bönpos* represent them as swastikas – the symbol of movement. The man with whom I spoke was a white *bön*. (...)
8. *Gyu*, written as *'rgyu'*: matter, substance.

9. (...) This means that the sound that can destroy the basic principle, the origin of the created world, is the fundamental sound, the subtle sound from which all destructive sounds are derived.

Part 2
History

'Don't you think so, Pooh?'
'Don't I think *what*?' said Pooh,
as he opened his eyes.
'Music and life...'
'Amount to the same thing', said Pooh.

Benjamin Hoff
(The Tao of Pooh)

The Origin of Things

The concept of sound as a medium which can transport the human spirit to a different state of consciousness is as old as mankind itself. It is a concept that can be observed everywhere, all the time, not only in man but also in animals. Wordless sounds transmit messages that are accompanied by states ranging from tension to relaxation, uneasiness to a sense of well-being. Animals can attract each other or scare each other off, reassure or warn each other with sounds. Man is no different. Every mother is familiar with the communication between her and her newborn baby. She responds immediately to the baby's crying and her soft crooning lulls the baby to sleep.

This is not a 'discovery'; it is a fact of nature that can be utilized by anyone who has the ability to produce sound.

What might be indeed considered a discovery, is that some people, as well as some animals, can produce sounds using things other than vocal chords. To begin with, the body produces many other sounds: heartbeat, circulation, digestion. Objects outside the body can also make sounds, either independently or when they are used by man. They can be dropped, shaken, struck, blown into, or rubbed together. Each of these sounds has a specific effect; they can give you goose pimples, or just a pleasant feeling. They conjure up feelings and images.

In creation myths all over the world, sound is recognized as the source of all visible and invisible things. The sound is preserved in those things. Just as all created things have their own sound, they also sing their own song. The lama's explanation in Alexandra David-Neel's story is a clear example of this.

The realization that man is a part of this whole, and the search to stay in touch with this whole, was already being expressed in early cultures through the use of sound. This can be found in Shamanism, which is probably the oldest existing religion on earth. Shamanism itself is actually already removed from the fundamental principle that every man has perfect communication with himself and his surroundings, as well as with the supernatural. After all, the shaman is still capable of this communication, which others can no longer achieve by themselves. And a shaman can restore communication when it has been temporarily disturbed. To achieve this, the shaman makes intensive use of sound. First, with a drum and his voice, but also with rattles and wind instruments. Joska Soos mentioned as the first of the 'Six Shamanistic Axioms': 'Sound is the basic element.' Before the Shaman took over this function, thus isolating it out of the whole range of possibilities at man's disposal, every member of the group (clan, tribe) played an equal part in the ritual. Later, the shaman, medicine man or magician became the leader in these rituals. The aim was to allow everyone to experience his existence, to express his feelings, and to take his place as a link in the chain which connects from the first mythical beings, through his ancestors into the next generation. Through song, dance and drumming, he interrelated with the place where he was, the community and the natural world around him. He made contact with his own inner space, with its contents, and with visible and invisible space outside himself. He placated gods, demons, forefathers and natural spirits. He gathered his strength together and expressed his eroticism.*

In fact, we still speak of 'tuning in', to indicate that we wish to establish an intense form of communication. And if this communication does not happen, there is no 'sound' connection.

In establishing this delicately tuned relationships (to the gods, for example), people who seemed to have a definite talent began to perform special tasks. In addition to their daily duties, they became a leader, shaman, or jester. Later, the people who fulfilled these functions were gradually relieved of their daily work so that they could dedicate themselves wholly to their special tasks. In this way they became important, 'chosen', and the priesthood was a natural next step. Consequently they became specially consecrated priests, who

---

* What a dreadful language, which does not have a neutral pronoun for men and women alike. Ladies, please forgive me for using only the masculine pronoun. Using he/she/it and him/her does not solve the problem. It only emphasizes the distinction.

had to study for many years, sometimes had to undergo many tests, and often deliberately isolated themselves from daily life, to act as negotiators. The priest was no longer an ordinary person among other people, but became someone placed outside and above others, with the sole right to represent God on earth when necessary, and even assume that identity.

Just as there have always been discoverers who travelled round the world to see it with their own eyes, there have always been people who only try to follow their own perceptions and constantly strive to establish their own links between the inner and outer worlds. Many of them were burnt as heretics or put to death in other ways.

We now live in an age called the 'Age of Aquarius', which is characterized by a great wish to be freed from all tyranny. More and more people recognize that they themselves are responsible. They will not, anxiously or obediently, let external circumstances be imposed on them from above. They are seeking an inner communication with the worlds in and around them, with the 'Cosmos', a commonly used term. They no longer need the intervention of the priest, doctor or doctorpriest: the shaman. This is why there is so much interest in the different ways and means by which man can re-establish inner communication. That is why there is increasing interest in the fundamental way of achieving this, i.e., through sound.

Ringing Stones and Fountain Bowls

In Asia, the use of sounding objects is very old. For example, the Chinese Emperors had the right to the most beautiful 'ringing stones' – hard stones, such as jade, which produce a ringing sound when they are struck. The first great Emperors reigned from about 2000 BC. There are records of a Bronze Age culture in China in about 1600 BC, and archeological finds in Northeast Thailand suggest that bronze was already used there about two thousand years earlier. Such finds show only that bronze articles were made that long ago, but until even older objects are found, it is impossible to say how much further back in history bronze was being worked. It is clear that by the 6th century BC the Chinese were far advanced in the manufacture of metal alloys and in the working of metals, from which they made perfectly tuned bells. It is difficult to say how many of these bells were made before that time, until earlier finds can tell us more. It is obvious that no culture can suddenly, from one day to the next, produce a tuned bell that weighs more than one hundred pounds, let alone a bell that can produce two different pure tones, depending on where it is struck. There must be some previous history. The study of sound and the effects of vibrations was so advanced in the 5th century BC that so called 'fountain bowls' were made from that time. These are bronze bowls with very specific shapes and dimensions. When such a bowl is filled with the correct amount of water, and the handles attached to the side of the bowl are rubbed in a special way with the palm of the hand, a fountain of water rises up, and a humming sound is produced.

Bowls are still used in Japan, for example, as standing temple bells without clappers. They are made of a black metal alloy and produce a short, rather 'dry' sound. The singing sound of various metal alloys has been extensively used in the many different gongs found in Asia. The discovery that metal objects produce sounds was made all over the world, and certainly small, metal, skull-shaped bowls were known around 1100 BC. With these bowls, you can strike the 'forehead' by the nasal bone and the point of the 'temple' on the edge of the bowl to produce two distinct tones with an interval of exactly a major third apart. That is by no means a coincidence. In the art of singing harmonics (i.e., producing a higher note above a particular basic note by using different resonant cavities in the head and body), it has been shown that the interval of a third remains the same. The makers of skull bowls had already discovered that this is the result of the shape of the skull; the distance between the nasal bone and the temple bone produces a major third. These bowls are the oldest known objects which can be described as 'singing bowls'.

Singing Bowls, Chalices, Food Dishes...

The caravan routes of Asia not only transported goods for trade, but also served to spread knowledge and religion. Shamans travelled south via Mongolia, and Buddhism crossed the Himalayas from India to the north. Shamanism and Buddhism came together in Tibet. The original religion of Tibet was the shamanistic-animistic Bön religion. In the 7th century AD the famous King Srongtsen (or Srong Btsan) Gampo married two princesses, one from Nepal, and the other from China. Both women were devout Buddhists. Gradually, two new movements developed: Lamaism, which is essentially Buddhist, but reveals strong Bön influences, and the Bön religion, which is now a sort of shamanistic branch of Buddhism.

Both branches of Tibetan Buddhism make intensive use of sound in their rituals and meditations (see Part 1).

But if you ask a traveller in the Himalayas if he has ever heard singing bowls in a monastery, or if you ask a Tibetan if the bowls we know as singing bowls are, or were ever used as singing bowls, the answer is nearly always negative.

There are round metal bowls in photographs of temple interiors, and they look exactly like our singing bowls; but clearly they are used as chalices. Travellers return from Nepal with accounts of metal bowls with a golden colour which are used for eating.

But if they are only offertory dishes and eating bowls, why the sound? And who made them like that? There are various opinions about who made the singing bowls, but they all point back to the shamanistic tradition.

In the first place, there are accounts of travelling smiths which also dates back to this tradition.

But did these metal smiths make the bowls on their own initiative, or were they commissioned to make the bowls? Were the customers monks who had the required knowledge to determine the proportion of different metals for the desired result? The metal alloys must have been made using a very special process which modern techniques are still unable to reproduce...

There is also a theory that the monks themselves were the metal workers who made the bowls. But then why do the people of Nepal use them for eating? No one has ever seen the bowls made in the old way, either by lamas or by travelling metal smiths. Bowls are still made nowadays, but they are cast, and the old alloys are no longer used.

According to tradition, the bowls are made of seven metals: one metal for each of the planets:

gold	the Sun
silver	the Moon
mercury	Mercury
copper	Venus
iron	Mars
tin	Jupiter
lead	Saturn

All these metals produce an individual sound, including harmonics, and together these sounds produce the exceptional singing sound of the bowl. The actual proportions of the different metals vary in each bowl, and it seems that not all bowls are made of all seven metals. Sometimes more metals are used, sometimes fewer. Thus the true Tibetan bowl is said to be made with more silver and tin, giving it a dull, anthracite lustre, while Nepalese bowls have the familiar golden glow.

However, the explanation for the differences in composition could also be that the travelling metal smiths did not carry their raw materials with them, but used the ores available in a particular area, which often contained several different metals.

The mountains and plateaus of the 'roof of the world' are richer in metal ores than in clay. That is why eating utensils were made mainly of metal or wood for a long time.

We can only try to reconstruct the method used to make a bowl from the original alloy, but it was probably as follows: the liquid metal was poured out onto a flat stone and left to cool as a metal plate. Then this plate was beaten with a hammer into the shape of a bowl, of which the metal was under maximum tension without cracking.

The inscriptions, decorations and other patterns which sometimes decorate the metal, were then punched into it.

Probably the customer could order a bowl with a specific sound or other quality. There would be a number of bowls, all of which would have roughly the same sound, but with slight differences in the balance of sound and the harmonics. The customer would make a choice from the bowls that were all of good quality.

This could explain why there are still so many bowls in circulation, even though they have not been made in the traditional way for the last forty years.

Another explanation is that many singing bowls were sacrificial dishes, and these were always very common in Tibetan monasteries. The fact that they have a special sound is because a gift offered in a sacrificial dish must also be harmonious in every respect. Therefore dishes must have a pure sound even though they are never rung out loud.

This does not mean that bowls were not also used as eating dishes. It is possible that the alloys of the bowls supplied homeopathic potencies of essential minerals in the diet. For example, a woman who had just had a baby would eat from these bowls for a whole month. But, if the bowls were really made by nomadic metal smiths/shamans, and if they were used in monasteries behind closed doors, then there are good reasons for everyone to keep silent about their shamanistic, singing use and to answer queries with 'I don't know' or dismiss them as 'eating bowls'. Buddhism is the dominant religion in the Himalayas where these bowls are found. Singing bowls are not used in 'official' Buddhist rituals. No one will openly admit that they own these objects which imply the practice of shamanistic rituals. For centuries even people in Christian countries have had to hide the fact that they are still using pre-Christian rituals. But everyone needs dishes to eat from so you could always buy them openly and display them in your home ready to be used. No matter what they were used for...

There could be many reasons why these bowls have not been made for the past forty years in the way described. An eating dish made of metal is very difficult to clean. So where the dishes were actually used for this purpose they have been replaced by China and earthenware imported from China. If the dishes were used for sacrificial rituals, the Chinese invasion of Tibet was the reason. With so many monasteries being destroyed the demand for sacrificial dishes suddenly and dramatically ended.

Thus there is no longer such a need for new bowls. The existing bowls can meet the present demand. But with increasing exports, especially to the United States, the question arises how long that will continue. If there were to be a greater demand for new bowls (and the more the Western traders discover the bowls the more there will be a commercial demand for new supplies from the local traders) they would no longer be made in the traditional way. The nomadic smiths seem to have disappeared. The knowledge handed down to them is dying out with them.

Part 3
How Singing Bowls Work

Every atom constantly sings a song, and it
is this tone which creates finer or denser
forms of greater or smaller density.

Lama Govinda

External Characteristics

When you compare a number of singing bowls by placing them next to each other, it is obvious that there are many different shapes and sounds. Most bowls are more or less golden in colour. They are round, but the ratio of the circumference and the depth varies. There are fairly shallow, broad dishes, which are small or medium in size. There are round bowls which are deeper. There are bowls with a small base or with a broad base, and there are even bowls with a completely flat base and a small, straight side. Some bowls have a stand so that they have the shape of a chalice. They are generally quite small and are rather rare. Bowls with a so-called 'bottle' base, which stands up concave in the bowl, are mainly made in India. They are fairly thin, and produce a different sound from the bowls hereafter referred to as 'Himalayan bowls'.

The thickness and colour of the material used varies from bowl to bowl. Bowls with a shining gold colour made of fairly thin material, round in shape and fairly small are generally Japanese bowls. They often produce a clear sound, more like a bell.

The sound is determined by the shape and thickness of the material, as well as by the thickness of the rim. The colour has no effect on the sound. There are some bowls with remnants of a dull black layer of varnish, usually on the outside. This layer is meant to be there and does not interfere with the sound. If you buy a matt bowl and polish it, this can influence the sound. By polishing the bowl, you remove a thin layer of the material so that the thickness of the metal is permanently altered.

Most bowls are decorated in some way, for example, with patterns of rings, stars, dots or leaves. Sometimes there is an inscription on the

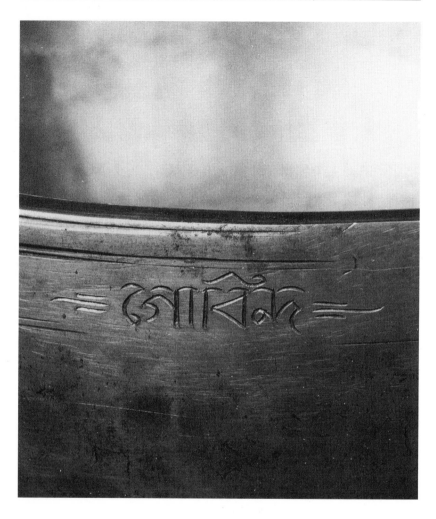

outside. This is usually in the Devangiri script which is used in Nepal, and indicates the name of the owner. Sometimes the writing is Tibetan, and this also refers to the name of the owner or the name of the ceremony for which the bowl was used. The Devangiri inscriptions suggest that singing bowls originated in Nepal and are only known as Tibetan bowls because the Tibetan refugees in Nepal earn their living by their traditional activities – i.e., trade. They traded not only the goods they brought with them, but also articles which they found in their host country.

In any case it is probable that the bowls with Devangiri inscriptions come from Nepal.

Decorated bowls may also be so-called 'calendar bowls'; for example, the decoration could be a lunar calendar or Jupiter calendar. The exact use of these calendar bowls is no longer known, but it is probable that the sound of the bowl and the movement of a few drops of water in it indicated which heavenly powers were present on that day, and which was the best day to use the bowl; thus it would only 'sing' its best on its 'own' astrological day.

The special knowledge and senses with which the influences of the celestial bodies can be calculated and used in all sorts of ways developed in other cultures as well as in Asia. For example, the Egyptian culture, closer to home, still presents a partly unsolved puzzle. The Celtic Druids also possessed this sort of knowledge and sensitivity. Perhaps singing bowls are a way of reviving these lost senses.

However, if you have your own singing bowl it will be difficult – and maybe even impossible – to discover whether it is really a calendar bowl (apart from making a guess based on the visible signs inscribed on the bowl) and to find out what planet the calendar is associated with, and how it can be used.

Some bowls, especially those engraved with patterns of rings, stars or leaves, may react like Chinese fountain bowls. When they are filled with water up to the engraved ring and are vibrated by striking or rubbing them, one or more fountains can rise up. If a star shape appears on the water, which then rises into a fountain from the middle, the bowl is called a 'star bowl'.

Sound is Shape

The wonderful phenomena mentioned in the preceding pages have a clear explanation.

Sound is vibration, and vibration is music in a three-dimensional form. Hans Jenny has taken superb photographs of sound shapes in water. Chladni spread fine grains of sand (or iron filings) on a sheet of glass or metal, and made the sheet vibrate by stroking it with the bow of a violin. The sand instantly arranged itself into beautiful geometric patterns, rather like a mandala. When the metal sheet was stroked in a different place, a different shape was formed.

When a surface is vibrated (a thin sheet of glass or metal or the surface of water), these vibrations spread in every direction in the same way. Because they are all produced in the same way, these waves are the same in whichever direction they spread. When two or more of these identical sound waves meet each other, they cancel each other out. The place where they meet is known as the meeting point.

The sand which lies on a vibrating sheet is shaken away by the vibrations. It collects in the places which are not vibrating – the meeting points – and in this way a pattern of lines appears. This looks like a two-dimensional pattern on the flat surface, but in reality the sound has a three-dimensional shape. The vibrations are transmitted in every direction – not just in the plane being vibrated. The three-dimensional shape of sound is visible in water. Water is a medium which can be vibrated very easily, and these vibrations travel over a large area. You can make a bowl full of water vibrate by rubbing or beating the rim; the vibrations will then spread over the surface of the water in every direction. If the vibration becomes more intense through prolonged rubbing or a special way of striking the bowl, the vibrations meet each other in such a way that the ripples literally raise each other up. The particles sometimes rise up several inches above the surface of the water. This can result in one or more fountains of small, sparkling droplets.

Natural Harmonies

In whatever way the people in the Himalayas may have used the bowls, one thing is certain: Western people are often affected in a special way when they first come across the sound of the singing bowl. Does this mean we cannot satisfy our desire for sound with the wealth of sound in our Western culture? Or should we ask: what is the difference, ultimately, between the sounds produced by the singing bowls and the sounds of our own musical tradition?

'Music' is not a chance phenomenon. Quite the reverse: everything can ultimately be traced back to music. The whole universe and everything that takes place in it consists of parts which relate to each other in the way of musical harmony. In other words: of all the theoretically possible connections and correlations which exist, the smallest known parts, as well as the largest visible parts, always choose proportions and connections which correspond to the intervals audible in music. Even these intervals are not chosen at random – of all the theoretically possible notes, the ones that are chosen have a particular ratio. For instance, if you vibrate a single string on a sounding-board, and then slide your finger along the string to gradually shorten the part vibrating freely, it should be possible, in theory, to hear the pitch going up. Actually the notes that are heard always change at regular set intervals. In other words, the whole universe, or to put it in simpler terms, everything in nature, arranges itself in musical proportions the way music itself does.

When a string is vibrated, it will produce its own basic tone, but above all it will produce a whole scale of resonating harmonics which include all the whole tones and semitones with ever-decreasing intervals. In Western music far less attention is paid to these harmonics than in the East. Bells, gongs, cymbals, as well as the bowls that come from Asia, produce far more harmonics than the musical instruments we use in the west.

Series of harmonics resonate at the natural intervals found throughout nature. They do not always sound harmonious to us. In 'music' based in the simultaneous sounding of different basic notes (chords), western Europeans use a system based on octaves. With two successive Cs the frequency (speed of vibration) of the higher note is exactly twice that of the lower note. They sound 'similar', and this applies for all the other notes – D, E, F, G, A and B – and their semitones.

The most harmonious interval to our ears is a fifth, i.e., two notes five notes apart. There is a perfect fifth, which has an interval of three whole notes and one semitone, and a diminished fifth, which comprises an interval of two whole tones and two semitones. Beginning on a C and progressing in perfect fifths, it takes twelve fifths to reach the next C . This cycle of twelve fifths is called 'a circle of fifths' . In a circle of fifths there are eight Cs, including the first and last C. This means that the circle consists of seven octaves. However if you calculate the frequency in numbers, you find that seven ascending octaves have a frequency of 128 together, while twelve ascending circles of fifths (there is a difference of 1.5 in the frequency of the lowest and highest note in a fifth) together have a frequency number of 129.75. So much for your perfect intervals!

In the 16th century a Chinese prince found the following solution: when instruments were tuned, the intervals were artificially shortened. A century later, J.S. Bach wrote 'Das Wohltemperierte Klavier', the first long, European composition that was based on this new principle of so-called even temperature.

Since then we have only heard music in which all the intervals are just too short in relation to their natural wavelength. Rational thinking has placed restraint on sound.

Gongs and singing bowls break through these artificial barriers. The natural vibration of the intervals between the harmony can be clearly heard. They sound different. They affect us differently. Sometimes free-floating sounds are experienced as unharmonious to the Western ear. In fact it would be more accurate to describe them as 'multi-harmony'. The sound comprises more subtle distinctions than you can hear in the calculated intervals of the well-tempered octave.

Synchronization and Inner Massage

Sound creates and sound arranges.

There is a third aspect which is just as important for understanding the effects of singing bowls and why they are increasingly being used therapeutically .

This aspect relates to the tendency of objects which make almost identical movements, to move completely synchronistically. Christian Huygens, the 17th century Dutch scientist noticed that when two pendulums were placed next to each other, they eventually started to swing in the same tempo. Similarly, after a while, two wave movements which are almost but not quite the same, change and become increasingly similar until they are exactly the same. This is called 'the collective arrangement of phases' or synchronization. Women are familiar with this phenonomen in their menstrual cycle. Friends or sisters who live in the same house often menstruate at the same time.

Many people feel that their spirit has been touched when they listen to the living sound of singing bowls. This feeling is less strong when the sound is recorded. Sometimes the sound instills a feeling of great space or profound peace. These and other experiences are not a matter of 'imagination' or 'belief' as people who have not experienced this phenomenon tend to suggest.

Furthermore, the sense of physical well-being after a singing bowl 'bath' is not only the result of relaxation.

We have already seen that water is an ideal carrier of vibrations. When you strike a singing bowl you can feel that the air surrounding the bowl also vibrates. People who have never heard of singing bowls and do not know what frequencies are, also experience this when they place their hand against a singing bowl for the first time.

The powerful vibrations spread quickly through our body, which consists of more than 80% water after all, and this results in a very delicate internal massage of all the cells. Physiotherapists also make use of this internal massage with ultra-sonic sound waves.

What is meant by the 'unification of phases'? The human body is a living entity of vibrations and wavelengths. A healthy organ is well tuned, meaning that it vibrates only at its own frequency, while the frequency of a sick organ is disturbed.

Singing bowls (as well as gongs and tingshaws) recreate the original harmonic frequency, and stimulate the body to rediscover its own harmonic frequency, by making it vibrate to the frequency of the bowl so that when it is synchronized, it can vibrate independently. Stimulated and taken up by the powerful vibrations of the singing bowl the body is able to tune into its own undisturbed frequency.

Shamanism and Brainwaves

In the shamanistic tradition, sound is seen as one way of entering into other worlds and realities. In the past the access to this other reality was an extremely well-kept secret and could only be achieved after a long period of study, meditation and special ceremonies. Well into this century all the teachings and information about what yogis and shamans did in these 'trance states' were generally considered as inexplicable 'secrets' or even 'miracles' or otherwise as clever tricks based on skillful suggestion and sometimes the superstition and credulity of the onlookers.

In the past ten or twenty years things have changed. The search for an 'inner self' or 'inner path' has led more and more people to look beyond the teachings of the Christian church. The signposts left by Jesus Christ have become obscured by the flood of dogma and liturgical discussion. The path of materialistic thinking seems to be heading towards a literal 'dead end' with the 'chemical death' of the environment.

Christian prayer has been replaced by Eastern meditation techniques and mantras have taken the place of the rosary. Sometimes it is necessary to adopt a new approach to remember and recognise the oldest principles. According to Joska Soos, the second and third shamanistic axioms are: 'The secret of all knowledge and the knowledge of all secrets lie in ourselves'.

In virtually every religion sound is used to take the spirit into another realm, where there is a greater receptivity for what is actually nameless and has therefore been given many different names: insight, light, God, the Self...

The Sufi master Hazrat Inayat Khan, who was a famous musician before dedicating himself to his task as a spiritual leader, said, amongst other things, that music not only gives people strength but can also transport them to ecstasy. He said that mystics throughout the ages have always loved music above everything else. Sufis have always considered music to be the source of inspiration for their meditations and believe that meditation with music is more fruitful than meditation without it.

The measurement of electro-magnetic brain waves has demonstrated that there are a number of clearly recognizable wavelengths, each connected with a different state of consciousness.

We know that in the normal state the brain produces *Beta waves*. *Alpha waves* are present in the brain in a state of meditation and calm consciousness. *Theta waves* are produced in a state of 'half sleep' and *Delta waves* are only activated during deep sleep.

It is also possible to record the waves produced by singing bowls. It was found that among the wave patterns of different singing bowls there is a measurable wave pattern which is equivalent to the alpha waves produced by the brain. These bowls, in particular, instil a sense of deep relaxation and 'inner space opening up'.

Information in the brain is transmitted through 'neurons', nerve cells with long branching offshoots which are connected to transmit nerve impulses. This transmission uses the electro-chemical properties of the cells to transmit rapid communication waves. Each of the ten billion neurons in the human brain has the potential for 100,000,000 connections. In fact the human brain has unlimited potential. It could be that the freely moving vibration produced by the singing bowls stimulate the neurons to make more connections. If that is the case, this could mean that consciousness is literally being increased.

Part 4
Practice

Even someone whose life is rooted in
knowledge acts according to his own
nature, because everyone behaves
according to his own character.
What then could men achieve by
oppression?

Baghavad-Gita 111.33

The Individual Sound is Always Unique

After reading the first chapters of this book you might think that you would need a great deal of knowledge to find a good singing bowl. Or you might spend a long time looking for a bowl with exceptional inscriptions because that sort of bowl is likely to produce the best sound.

In practice, people sometimes leave the decision to someone else. They may even say to the person selling the bowls, 'Find something for me, preferably a good matching pair.'

Of course, it is quite possible to do this. But these people are approaching the problem from the outside. Anyone who works with a 'bowl', whether he likes it or not, embarks on a journey to the inside, towards his own experience, his own harmony or whatever else you might want to call it.

Therefore the most natural way is that people will look for their own bowl. After all, everyone vibrates with their own frequency, and therefore they will only find their own bowl by listening to it themselves, not with their heads but with their hearts – and by feeling. Even people who are hard of hearing can enjoy a singing bowl. After all, the vibration is so tangible that it goes straight inside you, and the sensation is not diminished just because you cannot hear the sound. This is very clear with the sacrificial bowls; even though they are never sounded their wave patterns need to be harmonious so that the gifts for the gods are offered harmoniously.

Therefore it is not necessary to worry about finding a bowl which was obviously made as a singing bowl. Although some bowls do have a delightful sound, it is not really the 'beauty' of the sound that matters. There are bowls which sound dissonant, especially to the Western ear, but which nevertheless have a wonderfully liberating effect and these are bowls usually sought after by sound therapists. Anyone who is looking for his own singing bowl is firstly looking for a bowl that will 'touch' him. He is looking for the bowl that makes him take a deep breath and gives him a warm feeling flowing through his body. He feels carried along by the sound, and this is what attracts him. Feel it for yourself. Do not rely on another's judgement about the bowl.

Every person is a unique sounding board and will make the bowl resonate in a completely different way. That is why one bowl will resonate differently for different people. In addition, every person changes from one moment to the next, both physically and spiritually, and therefore the same bowl will sound different at different times. With some people the higher notes resonate longer, with others the higher notes fade quickly and the lower notes continue for a longer period.

Therefore you should not start by looking out for 'beautiful' or 'ugly' sounds in the usual sense of the word. Do not look for anything 'exceptional'. The sound of every bowl is unique, whether it comes from a small, unattractive bowl or from a magnificent bowl the size of a modest footbath.

The only difference is that if you buy the latter your 'own sound' will cost a lot more. Singing bowls are usually sold by weight. There is no point in quoting any prices here as these depend on the person selling the bowl and prices are changing anyway in the course of time. Pricing bowls by weight means that larger ones will be more expensive.

A Way to Choose

There are also different ways of actually choosing a singing bowl you wish to buy. There are people who know whether or not a bowl appeals to them when they have heard it sound just once. They are able to come to an intuitive decision quite quickly.

Someone who feels less certain but who still wants to decide on the basis of intuition can adopt the following method when choosing a bowl.

First place the bowl on a table with a cloth, towel or other light material between the bowl and the table. Place one or two fingers in the middle of the base of the bowl to keep it still. Now strike the rim of the bowl with a beater that is not too large, let the sound ring out and listen to the tone and resonance of the bowl.

If the bowl seems to be inviting you to a closer acquaintance, take it into the palm of your hand. Stretch out your arm so that you can easily hold the bowl in the hand in front of the body. Strike the bowl once again and let the sound ring out.

Now strike the bowl once again and bring it slowly closer to you. First, bring it near your stomach, a little below the navel. Strike the bowl again. Most importantly, do not listen to the sound with your ears but direct all your attention to your own body. What do you feel? What signals does the body produce as a reflection of the bowl's vibrations?

Take your time. If there is a negative reaction, no matter how slight, this is not a suitable bowl for you at the moment. This is not a judgement regarding the quality of the bowl or about your own personal situation. It merely means that you are not in harmony with this bowl.

If there is no rejection, strike the bowl again and move it upwards slowly towards the heart. Then stop, strike the bowl again and leave it to resonate. Again, check your body's reaction.

If there is no negative reaction repeat the process by holding the resonating bowl under your slightly jutting forward chin and then move it up to the base of the nose.

If you take the trouble to get to know a bowl in this way you have a good chance of finding one that is in harmony with you and your body.

If your body seems to reject the bowl strongly and perhaps even results in feelings of nausea, it might be better to forget the idea of working with singing bowls altogether. This does not imply anything good or bad or any other dualistic judgements. It only indicates that there are differences in people and the ways they walk.

If at any time you wish to buy a second or third singing bowl or even more, take the bowl or bowls that you already have with you, unless you have too many. But by that time you will know how to choose a bowl anyway. It is not necessary to have a series of bowls of greatly differing sizes. And it is impossible to assemble a 'singing bowl orchestra' with the melodious harmonies we know in The West.

The clear, floating sound of the singing bowl produces harmonies that are quite different from those that we are used to. By striking two or three bowls immediately after each other you can discover completely new harmonies and chords, and you will have a physical sense of whether or not they will appeal to you.

Tools

Singing bowls produce their singing tones in different ways. The first thing you will need is a 'gong beater'. The size of this beater depends on the bowl being struck. There are no real guidelines for this. 'Gong beaters' are beaters for percussion instruments, especially those covered with felt or fleece. It is a matter of trial and error, as every bowl has its own special requirements. One bowl will sound better with a softer beater, while others need a harder beater.

As a rule, a larger gong beater will produce the full richness of sound in a large bowl, while it is better to use smaller beaters for the smaller bowls. In fact, many different beaters can be used on any bowl. Every beater produces a different sound from the range of the basic note and its harmonics. Apart from the recognised gong beaters covered with felt, fleece, cork, rope or wood, you can use your own hands as percussion instruments – the heel of the hand, the fingers, the nails...

If you enjoy experimenting, you can try using almost anything as a beater. You can use just one beater or try working with two of the same shape. If you give full rein to your ingenuity and your love for playing the singing bowls, you will discover many surprises.

Another way to set the tones in the bowl ringing is to rub a hard stick around the rim of the bowl. This produces a similar effect to rubbing a wet finger along the rim of a crystal glass. A full singing tone is heard and steadily increases in volume. This accounts for the term: 'singing bowls'. According to some authorities, the former shamans of the Himalayas also used the singing bowls in this way to produce the singing sound. It is best to rub with a round stick or club made of hard wood. Again, the thinner the stick, the higher the tone that is

produced. Thus it is best to use a fairly thin stick on smaller bowls with a high tone.

It is extremely difficult to work on really large bowls with a thin stick. The vibration of the rim of a large bowl can be so great that the stick begins to 'dance' and this results in an unpleasant rattling sound.

You can prevent this rattling in several ways. You can press firmly and evenly against the rim of the bowl while you are turning it to prevent the stick from rattling. It is also possible to use a thicker stick. The pestle of a large wooden mortar could be very suitable. Finally, there is another technique which does not involve rubbing the stick around the rim of the bowl, but consists of rubbing it backwards and forwards in one particular place on the rim. It is often easier to use this method to produce a singing tone with a really large singing bowl.

With all these methods, the pressure and the speed at which the bowl is rubbed have an influence on the sound and the pitch of the tone produced. The penetrating singing sound that is created by rubbing the bowl is due to the fact that in this way one of the harmonics is accentuated and developed. To avoid the sound of wood on metal from becoming unpleasant many owners of singing bowls put tape on their sticks on the actual part that touches the bowl. This tape should be strong and smooth to avoid any abrasive sound and to prevent the tape being worn away by the rubbing. Clingfilm, such as the transparent sort used to cover books, also works very well.

This summary shows that really anything is possible. Many people make their own sticks for their bowls. I have seen sticks made of flannel wrapped around hard rope, sticks made of a long strip of felt boiled in starch and then wrapped tightly around the stick. Other rubbing sticks were covered with the inner tube of a bicycle or made from a wooden pan handle. Personally, I sometimes use the fork of a teak wood salad server set which, if it is used carefully, produces a marvellous, clear high tone with some of my bowls.

Signposts in a Magic Land

Anyone who owns his own singing bowl has access to a magic land of great ariety. There is so much to discover, to experiment with, to hear and to experience in the bowl and your inner self.

The way inward is open to you.

For more than a year I had only one bowl and it gave me great pleasure. It was all I needed. I constantly discovered new things and I had to assimilate what I had discovered. I still do not know all the possibilities this bowl offers.

Nevertheless, it is possible to put up some signposts in this magic land that will show the way along paths to be followed, even though every path is a strictly personal experience. These are some of the ways to work with singing bowls and to explore their possibilities step by step.

Listening
Listening to a singing bowl begins quite simply by sitting in a relaxed manner. Then hold the bowl in the palm of your hand, or put it on a firm cushion, a rubber ring (e .g. of a preserving jar) or on a soft cloth in front of you. Let the sound ring out. Listen to it with closed eyes. Start by experiencing the sound as a whole. Once you are familiar with the sound of the bowl, you can begin to listen to it analytically.

To distinguish the pitch of the various notes and to get to know and understand the nature of every tone, it is worth remembering that sound has a form and a wavelength. As you listen try to distinguish the pulse of the various tones. Is the sub-harmonic tone vibrating faster or slower than the dominant basic note? Do they harmonise easily with each other, for example by one being exactly two or three times faster than the other, or is the difference more difficult to measure: e.g., in a set amount of time, does one make five oscillations to the other's three?

By concentrating on one tone and, if necessary, following it with movements of the hand or body, it is possible to perceive not only different tones, but also different wave patterns in one bowl.

However, sounds not only have a wave pattern of straight lines, they also have a three dimensional shape. There are examples such as the expanding ripples caused by a stone thrown into still water, or the inner spirals of a whirlpool. You can discover these different sound forms by listening with your whole body and not just your ears.

You can also hold the bowl at different distances from your body, or even place it on different parts of your body, and listen again to see if you can hear a difference.

When you have tried all this, it is a good idea to stop analysing and allow the sound of the bowl to exist as a whole. Even when the sound has apparently died away completely you can still listen with the inner ear. Where has the sound gone? What do you hear in the ensuing silence? What is the sound of your own body? Of your essence? Of the silence?

Feeling

There are different ways of feeling the sound. If you place a singing bowl near or actually on your body you can feel the vibrations going through your body. One bowl may have a wave pattern consisting of large waves, another may have a sound which produces smaller, localised vibrations and yet another can give the impression of the sound going straight through your body. By lying down in a relaxed way and placing the bowl on different parts of your body, such as the stomach or chest, or even the head, you can observe the effects of the sound in as many ways as possible. Sitting in a chair you can try putting the bowl on your feet or thighs and knees. In this way you can feel the different physical sensations as well as the different sounds.

With larger bowls particularly, it is possible to feel the vibrations of the bowl when you hold your hand at some distance from the edge, where they are felt as a flow of warm air radiating from the bowl. When you are able to feel these vibrations you can try and sense the whole sound shapes around and inside the bowl. Another way of feeling the sound vibrations and absorbing them into your body, is to stroke the side of the bowl immediately after it has been struck.

It is also possible to touch the vibrating bowl with your tongue or lips. With closed eyes, and without touching the bowl with any part of the body, you can try and feel where the sound is vibrating most strongly, and what feelings are evoked in different parts of the body – feelings of release, relaxation, order or stimulation.

After these exercises and this concentration on the body's reception to the sound, it may also be helpful to return to the pure sound itself and to allow it to continue to sing without thinking or trying to analyse it in any way. Do exactly what the bowl does: set the air in motion. Breathe out strongly. Take a few deep, relaxed breaths. Experience and insight come to us particularly when we are able to let go...

Observing

You can clearly see the vibrations on the edge of a bowl that has just been struck. By observing this movement you will see different vibrations at the same time, and in this way discover something about the shape of the sound. With these exercises you can tune into the sound better, and you will be able to perceive the pattern of vibrations beyond the audible spectrum, even after the sound has ended. The sound of the bowl can be internalized to such an extent that it becomes possible to perceive the vibrations of the bowl just by looking at it and without even touching it.

Anyone who becomes so intensely involved with sound could, after a time, develop an inner experience of the relationship between form and sound and even see visions of geometric shapes: the shape of the sound imprints itself directly on the inner retina, without the intervention of a medium such as water, or sand on a sheet of glass.

Harmonics

A very special sensation can be achieved by using a technique in which the harmonics of the bowl resonate more strongly with the help of the oral cavity. When you sing a single note you can produce the harmonics by singing successive vowels with the same note and in this way moving the mouth cavity and tongue into the shape of each vowel.

By singing from A to O or from E to O in one breath, or just by singing a word such as 'boy' in one breath you can produce the harmonics, at first softly and gradually, with more practice, more clearly.

By placing the mouth near the rim of the singing bowl and allowing the mouth to form the vowels in the way described above, you can often separate out the different harmonics. To do this, hold the bowl at precisely 90° to the place where the rim was struck. Again, it is a matter of trial and error. This technique not only makes another aspect of the bowl's sound audible but it also has an internal effect. The vibrations reverberate in the body cavities, especially those in the head, throat and chest and this allows the sound to be experienced in yet another physical way.

Anyone who has learned to sing with harmonics, with a great deal of practice, can also try and sing a tone from the bowl aloud and then the harmonics above it. By doing this just above the edge of the bowl he will find that one of these harmonics will suddenly start to resonate in the bowl itself, and the sound of the bowl then directly reverberates in the body. It is almost impossible to describe this experience in which body and sound seem to melt into one vibrating unity...

Water

A simple way to make discoveries with a bowl is to fill it with water. Begin with a small amount and gradually add more. If there are any rings around the inside of the bowl these could indicate how full the bowl must be to produce the desired effect. But again discoveries are only made by experimenting.

By continually adding water to the bowl you can see what effect the water has on the sound produced and vice versa. First, rotate the bowl so that the water itself is rotating, and strike and rub the rim. Secondly, look at the patterns in the water in the bowl. It may actually be a fountain bowl.

Sometimes a bowl produces a beautiful, penetrating singing tone more rapidly by being rubbed if it is filled with water to a certain level.

Several Bowls Together

You can get to know a number of different aspects of a bowl, as described above. If you have several bowls there are obviously more

discoveries to be made. I would just like to mention a few more here. The most important discovery is what the bowls sound like together. What sound do they make when they are struck at the same time: can the sounds be distinguished, do they contrast with each other, do they harmonise? Do they cancel each other out (same wavelengths) or do they combine to create new sounds (connection of phases)?

By listening carefully, it is possible to get some idea of the wave patterns which are created when two sounds meet. Some bowls seem to produce the same sound at first but still you immediately feel that they are different. The difference can be discovered by listening intently. The difference can reside in the audible oscillations or in the harmonics, which may differ.

The reaction of one bowl to another varies from one pair of bowls to another. An example would be two bowls of about the same size which when brought into contact together create such strong harmonics that all kinds of tunes are created which can also be sung by forming the harmonics using the mouth placed precisely between the two bowls that are held close together.

I witnessed a truly remarkable pattern of co-ordinated vibration with two bowls when the larger of the two was placed upside down and the smaller was placed the right way up, on top of the larger bowl. When the smaller bowl was gently rotated it then started rotating of its own accord and the bowls together produced a strange, whistling, sliding tone.

An Open Heart and an Open Mind

It is worth repeating that singing bowls can give access to a field of unlimited possibilities, both by experimenting with them and through their internal effects. That is not to say that it is necessary, or even desirable to travel through this field in as many directions as possible. Firstly, the singing bowl is something we should enjoy, without any ulterior motives. Preconceived ideas of possible experiences will only be an obstacle to what is actually happening. If you are impatient to discover something, it can take a lot longer.

This means that anyone who expects something from sound will make the greatest discoveries by not expecting anything. An open heart and an open mind are, in the end, the most reliable signposts on the path leading inwards – both into sound and into yourself. When you hear something or experience something, in any form, it is important to take note of the experience, feel it and then let it go. Do not attach any great significance to it. Do not draw any particular conclusions. Remember that everyone undergoes changes and therefore influences sound in different ways. Most of the phenomena you have experienced, will recur. If they do not, then at least you will have enjoyed them without being attached to them, leaving the way open for more experiences.

Therapeutic Use

Singing bowls have an unmistakeable effect on people. Because of this they are increasingly used as therapeutic aids. We can only guess what the original makers and users of these bowls, whoever they may have been, would think about this. Although our 'holistic' way of thinking makes no distinction between the body and the spirit we still find it difficult not to make a distinction and to ignore the analytical thought processes we are so accustomed to using. On the other hand, the shamanistic approach of 'making no distinction', was a very different one. It was an approach that was not based on intellectual or rediscovered ideas, but was unformed and unspoilt. It was a natural approach which was simply experienced. We cannot think in these ways nowadays; we should not aim to do as they did. All we can do is to follow our own path, at the same time learning from the old traditions.

Anyone who feels the urge and intention to work with singing bowls for the benefit of others (as sound therapists or in combination with other techniques), following their own personal voyage of discovery into sound and its effects on the body and the soul, can find out about the different ways of working from practicing sound therapists and by being treated by them. Anyone who is interested in sound but does not necessarily want their own singing bowl may find that a treatment with sound or a concert or demonstration is a good introduction to the workings of sound.

Sound therapists also sometimes do workshops in which the perception of sound and the ways in which sound works are examined in greater depth. At these sessions like-minded people meet and can work together on the path of learning. They can make arrangements to use each other as subjects after the workshop to discover and try out ever more things together.

Later on, those who feel confident enough can gradually start to apply what they have learnt to their own family and friends. For the learning process it is important to choose volunteers who are prepared to tell you what they are experiencing at every stage. In this way the prospective therapist can assess what is happening and what effects have been evoked. At a later stage, when 'official' patients are being treated, it is not always possible to ask what is happening and what has been experienced. Many people cannot describe their experiences or prefer to assimilate them in silence. That is why exploration and practice are just as important in sound therapy as in any other therapeutic technique.

Part 5
Tingshaws, Bell and Dorje

'Farewell' said the fox. 'This is my secret, it
is very simple: You can only see well with
your heart. The essence of things
is invisible to the eyes'.

A. De Saint-Exupéry
(The Little Prince)

Tingshaws

If you go to a concert or massage with singing bowls, you will usually come across the penetrating singing sound of tingshaws.

Like singing bowls, these small cymbals, which are usually attached to either end of a cord or leather thong, are ritual artefacts. They are used by Buddhist monks but are also used in the Shamanist tradition. It is no longer clear who first used them but it is known that in general they are made of seven metals, just like singing bowls. In tingshaws the iron is replaced by meteorite, the 'celestial' metal which is taken from fragments of meteors and gives the instruments their pearly shine. Unfortunately, meteorite is a raw material which is only available in very limited quantities because of its very nature, and therefore not all tingshaws contain this metal. The final alloy is cast and turned to obtain a pure form and sound.

Tingshaws are available in different sizes, each with their own sound. Most are smooth, but there are also decorated tingshaws such as those with patterns of dragons and with the eight symbols of happiness, the Ashtamangalas. (See illustration on page 71.)

Meditational Use
The sound of tingshaws is like a summons. It brings man to the here and now. In meditation tingshaws are used to indicate the beginning and the end. At the beginning you let go of everything except the clean moment of here and now; at the end you should awaken physically and spiritually in the here and now of material reality.

In Tibetan Buddhist meditation rituals tingshaws are used in different ways. One way is as a summons: the Buddha, in one of his aspects, a deity or a spirit is summoned by the sound while the sound is also an offering to the summoned being.

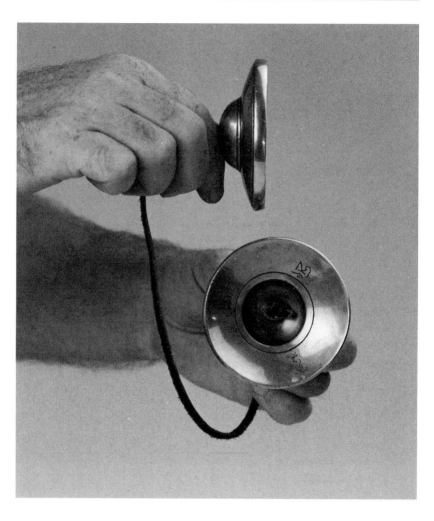

Tingshaws are tapped together at right angles for a loud penetrating effect.

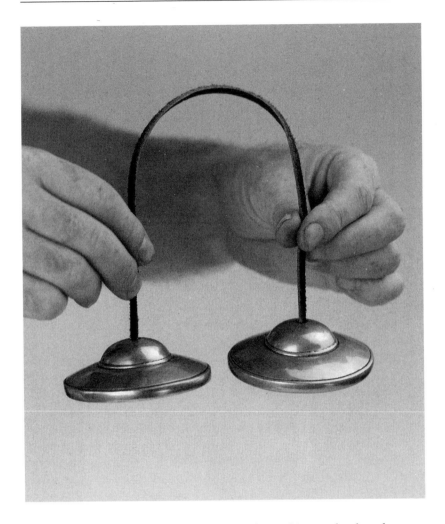

*Dangling horizontally, with the sides exactly touching each other, they pro-
duce a softer, light singing sound. They can also be tapped individually with
a hard wooden or metal rod. When you do this you can clearly hear the
minimal difference in pitch which tingshaws often have and which produces
the shimmering effect of the sound.*

Another use is in meditation exercises. Just as a master is meant to call back any pupil who has wandered off the path of a Zen meditation exercise, back to the here and now, by tapping him on the shoulders with a bamboo stick, the master in Tibetan monasteries calls a pupil who has wandered away back with the sound of tingshaws which are alternately sounded on the left and on the right, at right angles to each other, and then held with one of them upright in front of each pupil's eyes. Not only the pupil who has wandered but everyone else who is present is also immediately brought back to the centre of their meditation in this way.

Ritual Use

One of the very special uses of the evocative properties of tingshaws takes place in the ritual known as 'The Ceremony of the Hungry Spirits'. Very little is known about this ritual. Hans de Back describes it as follows:

'During his life, an unusual spiritual master had a tingshaw which is kept in a special little box after his death. This is a single disc on a plaited cord of silver, coral and turquoise with a piece of bone at the end (traditionally belonging to the deceased owner) which serves to tap the tingshaw.

The ceremony is as follows: a particular number of monks (4, 7 or 12) go to the banks of the lake. They sing harmonics and sound the tingshaw twice or three times. In this way they summon the spirit of the owner. It is not permitted to have direct visual contact with the spirit. That is why the monks wear special hoods over their faces so that they can only see the surface of the water and the reflections in it.

The spirit is probably summoned for a special spiritual lesson which enables the monks to consider their problems from a different perspective.

When the spirit wishes to break the contact, the monks sing sub-harmonics, which are so shimmering that they cause a wave to rise up on the water. The wave helps the spirit to separate himself from the earthly level to which he has been summoned'.

Therapeutic Use

Although we did not describe any specific therapeutic uses for the singing bowls, an exception should be used in the case of the ting-shaws for one special application of this pure and purifying sound. Nowadays we know quite a lot about auras, and what can be done for auras. When our body of flesh and blood, which we usually simply call 'the body' is disturbed, we know what we can do ourselves or who we have to go to for help. But a person does not consist only of his physical body and aura. There are several bodies. One of these is the socalled ethereal body. This is right next to the skin and many people can actually see it as a white, rather woolly outline slightly bigger than the physical body.

This ethereal body functions as a universal information filter. In other words, all outside information of any sort, is received by this body and passed on to the right place. In this way everything which comes to us from outside can be properly assimilated so that we can react to it appropriately. Someone with a whole ethereal body is always able to cope with anything which happens to him or her and to respond in a suitable way. He/she will have a great resistance to panic. When there are weaknesses or holes in the ethereal body, his/her reactions to external stimulae can change considerably. They are slower or inappropriate and the person is more likely to panic.

Holes in the ethereal body are particularly caused by drugs (including so-called 'soft drugs') and certain allopathic medicines such as antibiotics. The ethereal body does have the capacity to heal but when the holes are large this capacity is also weakened and it will be a very long time before it is completely healed. Sound, particular the sound of tingshaws can be a great help in this. This sort of sound treatment can soon help to form a new network of connecting threads so that the holes are repaired more easily and quickly.

People who have been treated with different tingshaws in a special order of sounds, feel better straight away and more comfortable and 'woolly' in their body.

Another useful application of tingshaws is based on the purifying effect of the sounds. By sounding the tingshaws in the four corners of a room, the energy present in the room is dissolved in the vibration of sound, and the room is once more 'open' and neutral.

Bell and Dorje

The bell is an instrument which summons the spirits and deities in the same way as tingshaws. In Shamanism, bells are used to summon spirits: their sound represents the element of air, the realm of the spirits. In Buddhist pujas (prayerservices) the bell is sounded at the moment that the form of the Buddha for which the ritual is held, is present in the room. The sound of the bell is seen as an offering to the Buddha.

Bells are made of bronze, often containing silver; the sound is partly determined by the silver content of the bell. The choice of the sound is a very personal matter. As a lama told me: 'You must go by the feeling of your own heart'.

However, anyone who sees the bell only as an instrument of sound, is missing its greatest significance in the Tibetan Buddhist tradition, usually in a symbolic unity with the dorje.

To understand this we must first know a little more about Buddhism.

The centre of the Buddhist philosophy concerns the 'Four Noble Truths': 1) man suffers, because he is attached to earthly existence; 2) the causes of suffering are desire, hatred and ignorance; 3) suffering can be relieved; 4) this can be achieved by destroying its cause. Every person can achieve enlightenment by following the right path.

In fact, every Buddhist school is part of one of the three main movements or 'vehicles': Hinayana, Mahayana and Vairayana or Tantrayana. In Mahayana and Tantrayana it is assumed that total salvation can only be achieved when every living being has been enlightened. Anyone who seeks enlightenment does so for the benefit for all living creatures. Lamas are the human enlightened guides on this path. Representations of Buddhas (principles of enlighten-

ment), transcendental Bodhisattvas (physical aspects of help and compassion) and gods (the personification of all aspects of human nature) serve as a support. They are accompanied by a multiplicity of symbolic objects.

The combination of method and wisdom is a basic principle of Tantrism. The method is seen particularly as compassion, wisdom as the consciousness which can conceive of the void. This term the 'void' means that nothing stands alone. Everything we perceive exists only because there is something which causes it.

The bell (Sanskrit: ghanta; Tibetan: dril bhu) and the diamond sceptre or thunderbolt (Sanskrit: vajra; Tibetan: dorje) are the symbols of wisdom and method. The dorje is a symbol of the indestructible, the male principle, the means of salvation. The bell is a symbol of the void, the female principle, wisdom. When these two come together, an inner mystical unity is achieved.

In puja (group prayer, offertory service) and sadhana (individual method of self-realization), the bell and dorje are used in the ritual gestures, the mudras. When the person performing the ritual wishes to express inner mystical unity, he crosses his hands at the level of his heart in the mahamudra, which expresses a state of being which embodies the most complete enlightenment. (Maha = large, mu = void of wisdom, dra = everything. Mahamudra is usually translated simply as 'large symbol'.) In Tibetan, it is usually called 'Tab Sherab'. Tab is the meditation of insight into the void, expressed by the bell; sherab is the meditation of the skilled method, expressed by the dorje. In the Tantric tradition, the dorje and the bell are actually specifically tools of the lama, because only a lama with a high level of self-realization permanently resides in Tab Sherab, and only a lama can transmit this mystical state to other living creatures. It is only when a pupil has received sufficient initiations from the lama on the path of enlightenment, that he may use his own bell and dorje, according to the Tantric tradition. It is assumed that merely holding the sacred objects does not have any effect at all; the effect is achieved only when the heart is able to assimilate the symbolic significance and make room for it.

Anyone who is attracted by the pure sound of the bell, and has bought one to use it as an object for meditation, can at least try to assimilate this symbolic significance as much as possible. The void is symbolized by the sound. In fact, this sound is not an independent entity, it is only created when there is a bell, a clapper and someone who brings the two together. The sound follows from this contact. Therefore the sound is created from the void and then disappears into the void. This is an exercise you could do with the bell: empty your mind, so that everything that is in it falls away. When your mind is as empty as possible, sound the bell. Listen how the sound is made, how it resonates, and how it finally ends...

The bell and dorje are only external symbols of an inner state of being, but their appearance itself is also symbolic; every part has a

In Shamanism, the bell is sometimes sounded by rubbing a stick round the edge; this produces a high singing tone.

meaning. These meanings are briefly summarized on the following pages. For a more detailed description of all the aspects concerned, refer to 'The Book of Buddhas', which includes a complete survey of the five 'Buddha families'.

Dorje

In a so-called 'peaceful' dorje, the ends of the spokes come together; in an 'angry' dorje, the spokes are separate. Ritual objects such as the bell, dagger and hatchet have a handle with one knob of a dorje; individual separate dorjes have two knobs; there are also double dorjes (visvavajra) with four knobs, but these are rare and almost only found in illustrations. The top half of the dorje represents the male side; the bottom half is the female side.

From top to bottom, we see the following aspects.

First, there are the five spokes, the symbol of the five Jinas (transcendental Buddhas), which represent the five forms of mystical wisdom. The four spokes on the outside each emerge from the open maw of a sea monster; this symbolizes the liberation from the cycle of reincarnation.

Underneath there is a hemisphere with eight lotus leaves, representing the eight Bodhisattvas.

The centre of the dorje is a globe, the symbol of synthesis, the point in which everything is enclosed.

The bottom half of the dorje is the mirror image of the top half. Here, the eight lotus leaves represent the eight dakinis (also called goddesses) of the Bodhisattvas, and the five spokes symbolize the five Buddhadakinis, or 'mothers'.

The Bell

The handle of the bell is the knob of the dorje, resting on a moon disc. Underneath there is a face.

According to one view, this is the face of the goddess or female Bodhisattva, Prajnaparamita, the incarnation of complete transcendental wisdom; according to another view, it is the face of Viarocana, the incarnation of universal truth, Dharma.

Looking at the outside of the bell from above, you see a mandala (illustrated in the circle on p. 72).

From the centre down to the edge, this contains the following components: a circle of eight lotus leaves, which forms the mandala of the voice of the gods, with the mantras of the five Jinas written in the leaves. There is a broad decorative strip all around this, which often contains dorjes.

The outer (bottom) edge is filled with exactly 51 dorjes, which represent the 51 small unknowns which can be resolved by the effect of the bell.

The sound mantra of the bell is the 'OM' ('AUM') sound, which symbolizes perfection and is seen as the sound of the body, voice and spirit of Buddha, as well as being a symbol of the voice of all the gods together.

Iconography
In the rich iconography of Mahayana and Tantrayana, the dorje and bell are common images. The dorje is often seen without the bell, and with other attributes, but the bell is rarely found without the dorje. For example, the Buddha Amitabha, in tantric union with his female partner (prajna) uses a bell and a begging bowl, in which an ashoka tree is germinating as a symbol of the carefree bliss beatitude of the interim paradise Sukhavati, of which Amitabha is the lord.

Buddha Amoghasiddhi uses the bell and the sword, the symbolic destroyer of ignorance in illustrations in which he is shown in tantric union with his prajna, Tara.

Some illustrations of Vairocana show the combination of the bell and dharmachakra (the wheel of truth).

Vairocana, who is sometimes seen as the original Buddha, is called Vajradhara when he is depicted in the classical mahamudra with the bell and dorje.

Vajrasattva is shown in a different position with the bell and dorje. In Nepal, this Buddha is seen as the original Buddha, who was there before all the others, the 'Lord who was created from himself'. In Tibet he is called 'Dorje Sempa', and he is seen as the essence of the body of all Buddhas. With him, the dorje and bell are symbols of perfect compassion and perfect wisdom, and his prayer is that of perfect joy. He is illustrated on the opposite page.

The Lama at Work

It is an exceptional experience to see the Lama at work with the dorje and bell. It is described in words of wonder and respect in many books about Tibet and Tibetan Buddhism. I shared in this experience when I visited Lama Gawang in Lelystad, the Netherlands. His magnificent bell and dorje, decorated with turquoise, were lying in front of him on a garden table in the sun. Lama Gawang explained to me what he was doing.

'The bell is the female side; the dorje is the male side. But the female heart points to the right, and the male heart points to the left; therefore we place the dorje to the left, and the bell to the right, in front of us.'

When the Lama performs this ritual for himself, the face on the bell is pointing towards him, but if it is meant for others, he turns this face away, towards them.

First, the dorje is picked up with the right hand, the male hand, and then the bell is picked up with the left hand, the female hand. The Lama's hands described beautifully stylized arcs, in which the dorje and the bell constantly changed position in an easy, flowing movement.

The Lama explained: 'The movements of the hands symbolise the activities of the gods while they are dancing.' My attention was completely taken up with the dance, but the movements were over before I had a chance to see them properly.

The Lama crossed his hands over his chest with a light, serene smile. He said: 'The dorje is held slightly higher than the bell. This is Tab Sherab. Tab makes the ego smaller; Sherab purifies it. When the ego has gone, all suffering is dissolved. It is the work of the Lamas to perform this; it is the work of the pupil to meditate and take the power from the ego.

The Lama is the guide. Tilopa, the founder of our order of the Kagyupas, said to his pupil: 'I have shown you the way how to go to the Buddha. But you will have to go yourself.'

Conclusion

Only the sound –
but then it was an evening
of summer rain

Issa
(Japanese Haiku poet)

The water in the bowl gleams.

I strike the rim of the bowl softly at first and then slightly harder. At first slowly, but then in faster cadences...

The water in the bowl is ruffled in a fine herring-bone pattern; the same endlessly repeated pattern that is engraved on the side of the bowl.

Suddenly the miracle happens again. Drops of water shoot up in four places, higher and higher, until the round, silver drops spray out several inches above the rim of the bowl and then fall back into the bowl with a clear, splashing sound accompanying the familiar singing of the bowl, with their sparkling sound.

I do not know where this bowl came from, when it was made, by whom or why. After much study and research I still do not know. I do not know whether the maker meant to create these delightful effects when he shaped the bowl, with the hammer blows that are still visible, and when he engraved the decorations and applied the matt black layer of varnish which is now half worn away.

Perhaps he would laugh in bewilderment if he saw what I was doing. Perhaps he would be happy that his work was still being used. Perhaps he would think I was stupid because it is so obvious that I do not understand. But why should I care?

What is important, is the sound...

Sources and Bibliography

Hans de Back – Danny Becher – Lisa Borstlap – Erik Bruijn – Binkey Kok – Dries Langeveld – Joska Soos.
With thanks to **Ronald Chavers** for the many years of teaching on Shamanism.

Lao Tse: Tao Te Ching
Mirananda. The Hague, 2nd edition

Inayat Khan: Music and Mysticism, Sufism and the harmony of the spheres
Servire Uitgevers B.V., Katwijk aan Zee 1987

Erik Bruijn: Tantra, Yoga and Meditation, The Tibetan path to enlightenment
Ankh-Hermes b.v., Deventer 1980

Alexandra David-Neel: Tibet: Bandits, Priests and Demons
Uitgeverij Sirius en Siderius, The Hague, 1st edition, March 1988

Benjamin Hoff: The Tao of Pooh
Uitgeverij Sirius en Siderius, The Hague, 3rd edition, February 1987

Joska Soos: I am not healing, I am restoring harmony
Compiled and arranged by Robert Hartzema
Uitgeverij Karnak, Amsterdam 1985

Robert K.G. Temple: China, 3000 years of inventions and discoveries
Van Holkema en Warendorf 1988

Joachim-Ernst Berendt: Nada Brahma: The world is sound
A quest through music, development and consciousness
East-West Publications, The Hague 1988

Terence Dixon/Tony Buzan: The Brain
Zuidgroep b.v. Uitgevers, The Hague 1979

Bhagavad-Gita
The Bhaktivedanta Book Trust, Amsterdam, 2nd edition

J. van Tooren: Haiku, A young moon
Meulenhoff, Amsterdam 1973

Tarthang Tulku: Hidden freedom
Uitgeverij Karnak 1983

Lama Lödö: Bardo, the path of death and rebirth
Uitgeverij De Driehoek, Amsterdam 1989

Frans Boenders: Tibetan diary
Uitgave van BRT, Brussels, 1987

A. de Saint-Exupéry: The Little Prince
Uitgeverij Ad Donker, Rotterdam 1980
BRES 120, Oct-Nov, 1986
Dries Langeveld: The mystery of the singing bowls

PRANA 53 Autumn 1988
Theme issue: Music and Music therapy

ONKRUID 61, March/April 1988
Page 63-101: Music, ceremony and sounding spirituality

The character which marks the last pages of the different parts of this hook, is the symbol of the universal soundmantra **OM**.

Also published in this series

Eva Rudy Jansen

The Book of Buddhas
Ritual Symbolism used on Buddhist Statuary and Ritual Objects

A brief introduction to Buddhism is followed by a lengthy survey in words and images of the most common figures, positions and symbols in Mahayana and Tantrayana Buddhism. Each individual item is clearly illustrated and accompanied by a short description of its significance. Though it does not pretent to be complete, this book is nevertheless a valuable work of reference, providing anyone who is interested with an overall iconography of a world religion and its accompanying imagery, of which the philosophy and artistry have gradually also penetrated the west.

ISBN 90-74597-02-5

Eva Rudy Jansen

The Book of Hindu Imagery
The Gods and their Symbols

Hinduism is more than a religion; it is a way of life that has developed over approximately 5 millennia. Its rich history has made the structure of its mythical and philosophical principles into a highly differentiated maze, of which total knowledge is a practical impossibility. This volume cannot offer a complete survey of the meaning of Hinduism, but it does provide an extensive compilation of important deities and their divine manifestations, so that modern students can understand the Hindu pantheon. To facilitate easy recognition, a survey of ritual gestures, postures, attires and attributes, and an index are included.

ISBN 90-74597-07-6

Ab Williams

The Complete Book of Chinese Health Balls
Practical Exercises

This book deals with an ancient Chinese fitness technique that has been in use since the Ming Dynasty (1368-1644). Two, usually metal, balls are to be moved around in the palm of the hand, thus stimulating the nervous system. These health balls are believed to improve memory, stimulate circulation, relax the muscles and tune the chi (life energy). In this book you will learn about chi and the nervous system and you will find a wide range of practical exercises that will enable you to optimise your energy. The author discusses the historical backgrounds, gives a survey of the different types of balls and their characteristics and takes you step-by-step through the basic exercises, walking and meditation exercises, and teaches you how to use the balls for massage and for strengthening and balancing the yin/yang energy in your body.

ISBN 90-74597-03-3

George Hulskramer

The Life of Buddha
From Prince Siddharta to Buddha

There are few histories of Prince Siddhartha that are as accessible to all ages as this one. In comic-book format, Hulskramer tells the colorful story of the Buddha Siddhartha, skillfully illustrated by Nepalese artists Raju Babu Shakya and Bijay Raj Shakya. This is a readable biography for anyone who is interested in Buddhism, a wonderful, exotic fairytale for lovers of beautiful illustrated stories, and a collector's item for cartoon enthusiasts.

ISBN 90-74597-17-3

Anneke Huyser

Singing Bowl

Exercises for Personal Harmony

Did you know that you have your own basic tone that you
vibrate every day, and that your tone changes as your life
changes? It's a fact that sound is energy. With the right
information, and practice, you can use the vibrational energy of
singing bowls to adjust, restore, and maintain your personal
harmony.

Anneke Huyser explains the symbolism of the bowls and
beaters, how their metals correspond to the planets, and how
planetary energies, reflected in the frequencies of certain
bowls, can be harnessed for personal transformation. She also
provides information on the frequencies of colors so you can
combine sound with color therapy principles, and she includes
basic information about the body's seven major chakras and
how they are affected by singing bowls. With the exercises
provided here, you'll learn how to:

- retrain how you listen to sounds;
- find your basic tone and choose a bowl that matches your
  personal frequency;
- make your bowl sing;
- work with planet tones;
- experience the healing vibrations of the bowls
- give or receive a singing bowl sound massage;
- use singing bowls in storytelling and many other activities.

Whether you own one or several bowls, or just enjoy listening
to them in recording or live perfomances, with this book you'll
gain a deeper appreciation for these lovely instruments.

ISBN 90-74597-39-4

CD's and Cassettes with Singing Bowls:

Hans de Back: **Singing Bowl Meditation 1 –
Music for Relaxation and Meditation**
CD: ISBN 1-57863-058-4
MC: ISBN 1-57863-059-2

Rainer Tillmann: **The Sound of Planets 1 –
Meditations with the Planet Sounds of
Tibetan Singing Bowls**
CD: ISBN 1-57863-063-0
MC: ISBN 1-57863-064-9

Rainer Tillman: **The Sound of Planets 2 – Nada**
CD: ISBN 97-81-578-630-653
MC: ISBN 97-81-578-630-660

Rainer Tillmann: **Sabda – The Purity of Sound**
CD: ISBN 1-57863-060-0
MC: ISBN 1-57863-061-4

Rainer Tillmann: **Chrystal Sounds – Deva**
CD: ISBN 97-81-578-630-707
MC: ISBN 97-81-578-630-714

Rainer TIllmann: **Sounds for Healing 1 – Soma**
CD: ISBN 97-81-578-630-684
MC: ISBN 97-81-578-630-691

Hans de Back: **Gong Mediation 2**
CD: ISBN 1-57863-054-1
MC: ISBN 1-57863-055-X

Hans de Back: **In Concert**
CD: ISBN 1-57863-056-8
MC: ISBN 1-57863-057-6

Hans de Back: **Singing Bowl Chakra Meditation**
CD: ISBN 1-57863-052-5
MC: ISBN 1-57863-053-3

Distributed in the U.S.A. by Samuel Weiser Inc., Box 612,
York Beach, Maine 03910-0612
Orderphone: 1-800-423-7087